This book belongs to

· ·

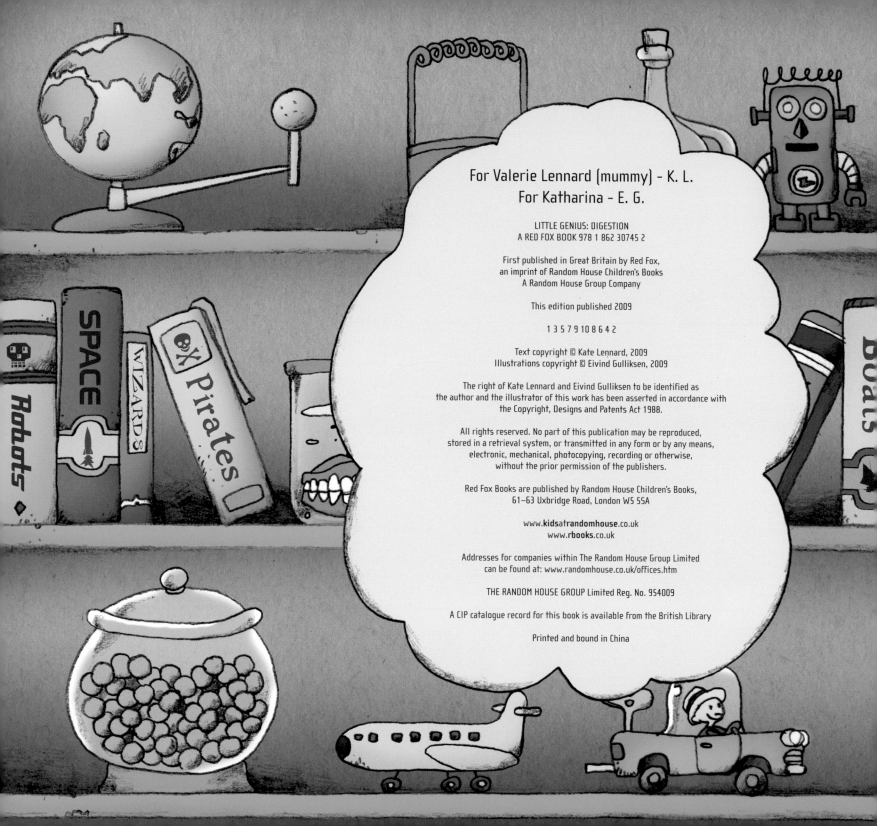

For Valerie Lennard (mummy) – K. L.

For Katharina – E. G.

LITTLE GENIUS: DIGESTION
A RED FOX BOOK 978 1 862 30745 2

First published in Great Britain by Red Fox,
an imprint of Random House Children's Books
A Random House Group Company

This edition published 2009

1 3 5 7 9 10 8 6 4 2

Red Fox Books are published by Random House Children's Books,
61–63 Uxbridge Road, London W5 5SA

www.kidsatrandomhouse.co.uk
www.rbooks.co.uk

Addresses for companies within The Random House Group Limited
can be found at: www.randomhouse.co.uk/offices.htm

THE RANDOM HOUSE GROUP Limited Reg. No. 954009

A CIP catalogue record for this book is available from the British Library

Printed and bound in China

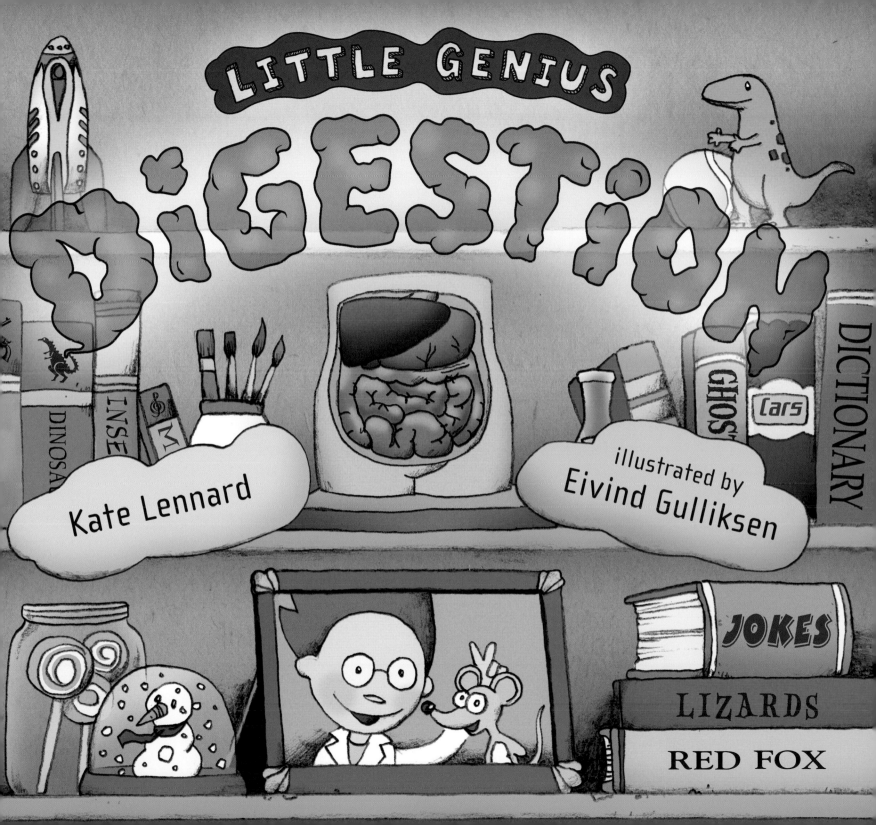

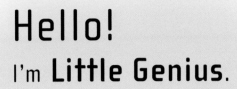

Hello!
I'm **Little Genius**.

I've been looking into the human body, and all the interesting bits that make it work.

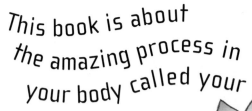

This book is about the amazing process in your body called your **digestion**.

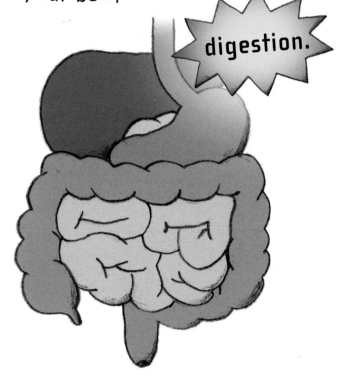

I'm here to tell you all about it . . .

Putting food in your body is like putting fuel in a car. If you don't fill it up, it won't work properly!

You need food to make energy, stay healthy and grow big. But before your body can soak up all the goodness, it needs to be turned into slop.

Nobody wants to eat slop! So your body does lots of clever things to melt it down.

This is called **digestion.**

Digestion starts happening the moment you think of something tasty. Your mouth goes watery and your tummy rumbles.

Dogs' mouths get so watery when they see something tasty, they dribble!

Can you think of anything yummy that makes your mouth go watery? That's your mouth juice getting ready to melt the food!

Look at this feast.

Is anything making your tummy rumble?
That's your tummy pipes
getting ready to make slop!

Once inside the mouth, food needs to be cut up, chewed and chomped.
That's what your teeth are for!

Mouth juice mixes with the food to help make it mushy. Your tongue shapes the mush into little balls that get pushed to the back of your mouth, ready for swallowing.

Have you ever tried to look down the big hole at the back of your mouth?

It's impossible!

So where does it go?

Let's have a look!

At the back of your mouth are two pipes. One is for breathing — it's called the **wind pipe**. The other one is for mushy food and drink — it's called the **oesophagus** (that's uh-soff-a-gus).

The oesophagus is no wider than a ping-pong ball. If you don't chew your food properly, a lump could get stuck!

oesophagus

mushy food

flap

wind pipe

A flap of skin covers your breathing pipe when you swallow to stop anything going down the wrong hole.

As each mush ball is squeezed along it gets squirted with more juice to help it go down. Count to 3 slowly. That's how long it takes!

When you drink something your body starts soaking it up straight away.
You're a bit like a plant that needs to be watered!
If you don't drink enough you'll dry up like an old leaf.

At the bottom of the oesophagus is a special ring that opens up when it feels a mush ball coming.

On the other side of the ring is a bag called your **stomach**.
This is where the slop gets made. Everything sloshes about and gets mixed with even stronger juices to give it a clean.

Stomach juices are so strong they could melt a coin! The stomach walls are covered in tummy slime to protect them from getting melted too!

Your stomach stretches out to fit in all the food. Eat too much and it will feel tight at the sides. That's what happens when you feel full up.

Food stays in here for about **4 hours**.
That's longer than morning at school *and* lunchtime!

When it's been there long enough it starts to dribble down into . . .

. . . the **small intestine.**

It's a really long tube squashed in underneath your stomach. Pulled out straight it would be as long as 22 footsteps!

22!

When the slop arrives, three important squashy bits send in special juices.

The first is called your **pancreas**.

It looks a bit like a leaf, doesn't it?

The second is called your **gallbladder**. It's a pear-shaped bag full of goo called **bile**.

The third is called your **liver**. It's the biggest squashy bit in your whole body!

These special juices turn the slop into a watery slush that can be easily shared out around your body.

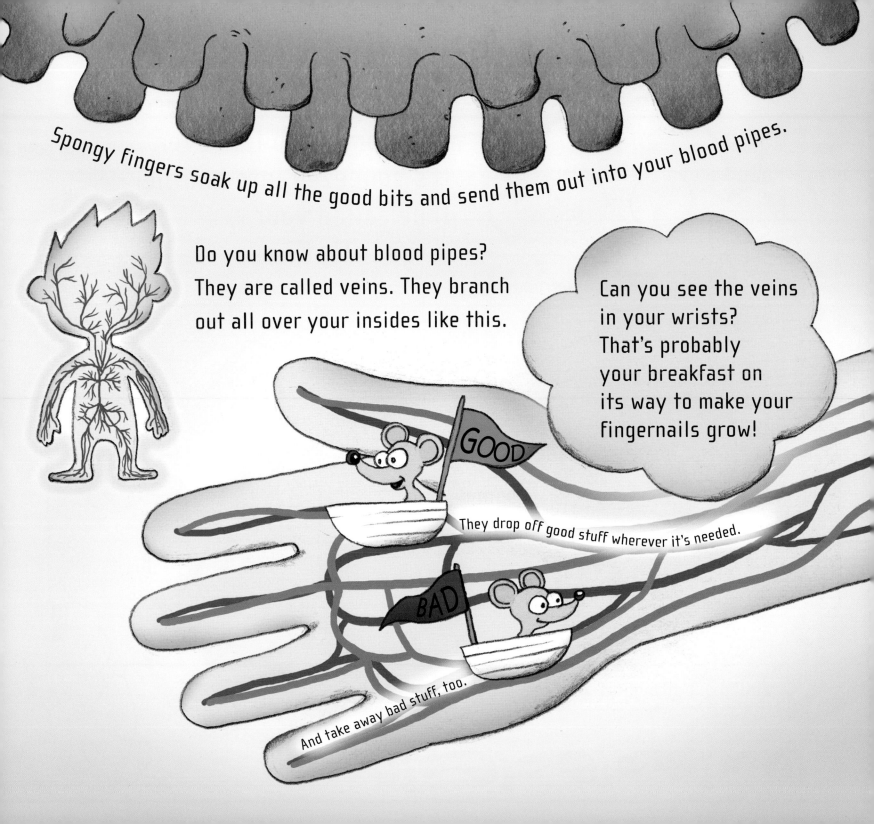

Spongy fingers soak up all the good bits and send them out into your blood pipes.

Do you know about blood pipes? They are called veins. They branch out all over your insides like this.

Can you see the veins in your wrists? That's probably your breakfast on its way to make your fingernails grow!

GOOD

They drop off good stuff wherever it's needed.

BAD

And take away bad stuff, too.

When all the good slosh has been soaked up there's still some slop left over. It's squeezed into another tube called your **large intestine**.

It starts here under your tummy button.

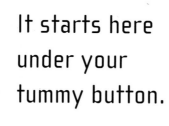

Pulled out straight it would be as long as five feet.

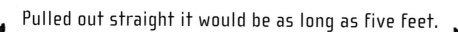

It's a very dry place. That's so any remaining water can be taken away and used somewhere else.

Your body needs as much water as it can get.

Slop stays here for a day or so, getting harder and dryer. It slowly moves along, making its way nearer to your bottom hole.

FLUSH!

This is where the dried-up slop waits to get dumped. That happens when you sit on the toilet. You squeeze it out and flush it away!

Let's have a look at your whole digestive system.
Can you believe how much there is to fit in?

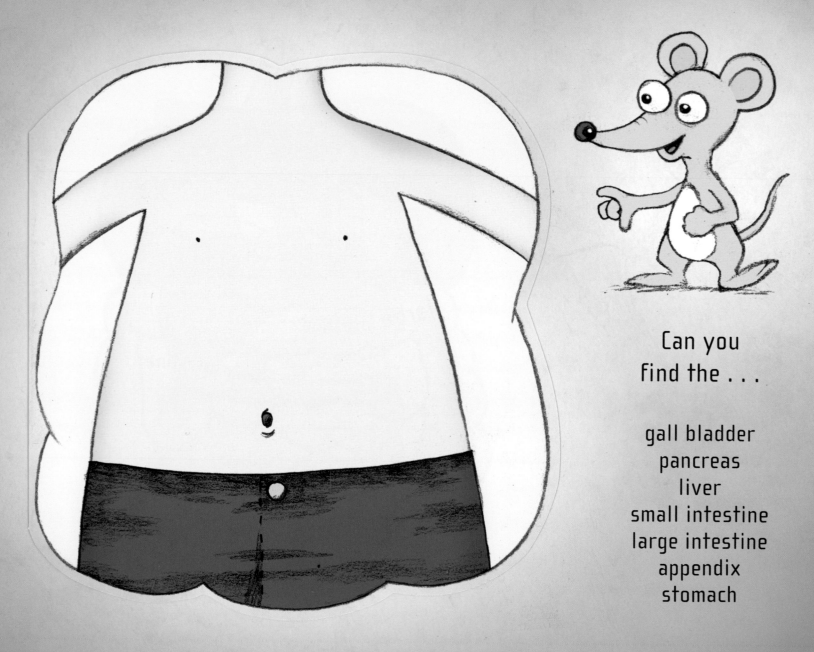

Can you
find the . . .

gall bladder
pancreas
liver
small intestine
large intestine
appendix
stomach

Sometimes things can go wrong with **digestion.**

Have you ever been sick? That's when your stomach throws food back up your food pipe before it's had a chance to digest it.

Sick is horrible. That's the tummy juice you can taste.

Another yucky thing that can happen is **diarrhoea**. That's when slop travels down your bottom pipes too quickly and doesn't have time to dry up properly.

Sometimes a poo takes a long time to come out. Your tummy feels full up and very uncomfortable. It's called being **constipated**.

To stop it from happening to you, eat lots of fruit and vegetables and drink plenty of water.

If you swallow any air when you eat, it can pop back up and out of your mouth! Air can come out of your bottom tubes too!

BURP!

Bottom burps can sound very rude!

POP!

POP!

POOH!

Did you know that the bubbles in fizzy drinks are actually air balls? Drink too many and you could get a very windy bottom!

Some more interesting facts about other animals' digestive systems.

Plant-eating animals like zebras and giraffes need to eat all the time. It's called **grazing**. That's because plants are hard to digest. They get pooped out before all the goodness has been soaked up.

Can you think of any other animals that graze?

Hippos don't have front teeth,
They chew with their top lip instead.
Can you pretend to eat like a hippo?

Worms chew up old leaves and roots and poop it out as fresh soil!
Now that's what I call recycling!

I'd quite like to be
a gastroenterologist
when I grow up.

Would you?

More **Little Genius** books
for you to enjoy

EYES

9781862307476

BONES

9780099451631

BRAINS

9780099451624